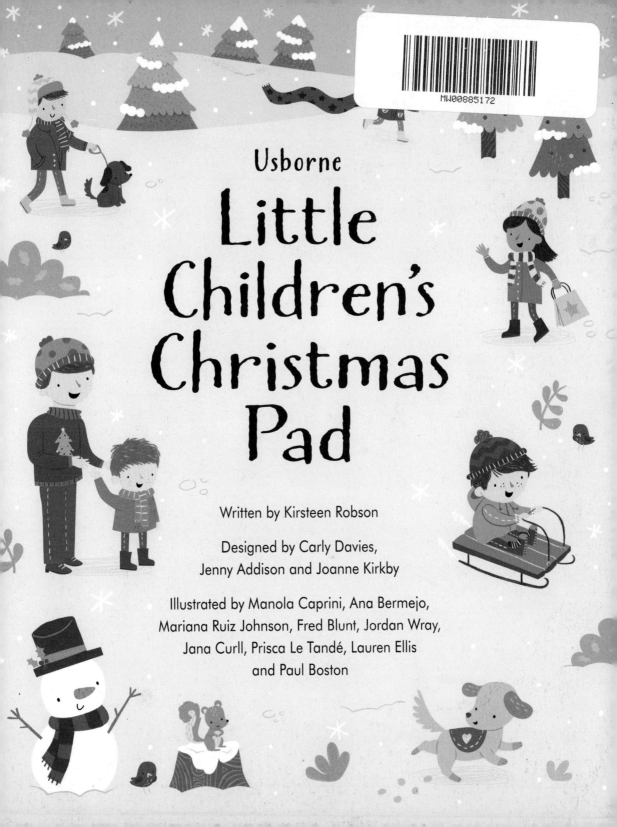

Usborne

Little Children's Christmas Pad

Written by Kirsteen Robson

Designed by Carly Davies,
Jenny Addison and Joanne Kirkby

Illustrated by Manola Caprini, Ana Bermejo,
Mariana Ruiz Johnson, Fred Blunt, Jordan Wray,
Jana Curll, Prisca Le Tandé, Lauren Ellis
and Paul Boston

Circle the picture that has just been taken.

A

B

C

Lead Bunty and Ben to the elf village.

Are there more people with elf hats or antlers on their heads?

Santa's Grotto →

Answer:

....

Spot 4 differences.

Find and circle these things in the big picture.

Are there enough carrots for each reindeer to have one?

Answer:

....

Find and circle three elves wearing matching clothes.

Find and circle the stall that Keira will go to.

Keira

It has Christmas lights...

...a green roof...

...and it does not sell food.

Draw a line between each puppy and its parent.

Find the hidden words. They may be written across or down. One has been found for you.

r	o	u	n	w	p	e	i	f
a	n	n	f	r	e	e	z	e
b	i	r	d	x	p	n	f	e
b	d	s	x	o	a	x	r	t
i	x	s	n	o	w	c	e	b
t	r	a	c	k	s	a	o	z
f	o	x	a	y	s	m	d	i
z	e	w	t	t	l	g	e	p

cat ✓   feet   freeze
fox   paws   rabbit
bird   snow   tracks

Draw around these two groups in the picture below.

1.

2.

Circle the angel that matches this shape.

14

Draw a line down the channel with the fewest seals.

Find and circle...

16

...a penguin in a hat

...an angel

...a pair of
red mittens

...and a mouse.

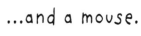

Spot 4 differences.

Write 1, 2, 3 or 4 on each picture to put the story in order.

. . . .

. . . .

. . . .

. . . .

Lead Billy up to the window to fix the bulbs that are not lit. He can't go up broken ladders.

Billy

Find and circle Charlie the elf.

Charlie is wearing green boots...

...a striped hat...

...and has brown hair.

Are there more mice or rabbits?

Answer: ....

Draw antlers on the reindeer.
One has been done for you.

Find and circle enough hats, carrots and scarves to finish the snowmen.

Follow the trails to see which house Santa will visit next.

26

Find and circle the penguin that is facing the wrong way.

Find the hidden words. They may be written across or down. One has been found for you.

28

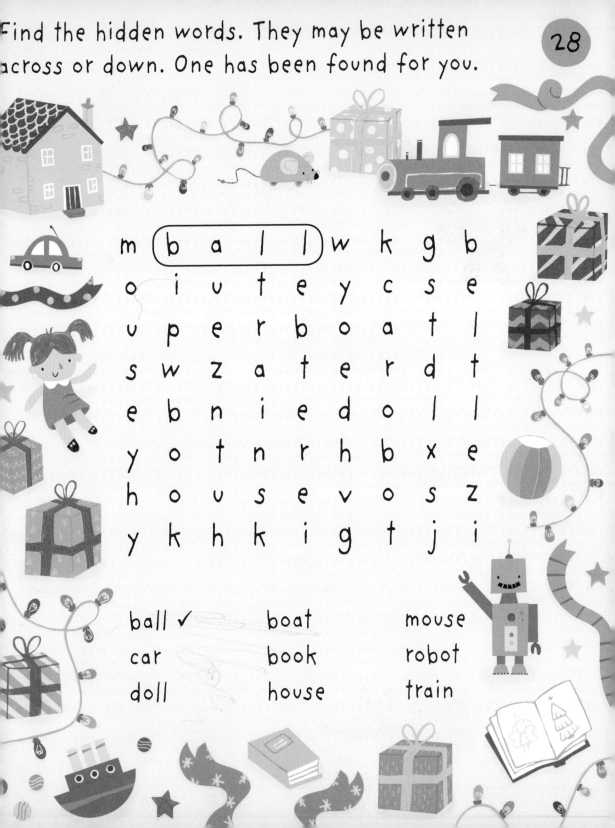

m	b	a	l	l	w	k	g	b
o	i	u	t	e	y	c	s	e
u	p	e	r	b	o	a	t	l
s	w	z	a	t	e	r	d	t
e	b	n	i	e	d	o	l	l
y	o	t	n	r	h	b	x	e
h	o	u	s	e	v	o	s	z
y	k	h	k	i	g	t	j	i

ball ✓   boat   mouse
car   book   robot
doll   house   train

Lead Santa along the path to Rudolph the red-nosed reindeer.

Find and circle...

...an umbrella

...a reindeer

...a dog

...an elf

...and an ice-cream cone.

Draw a line along the icy path without touching its edges.

Circle the piece that will finish the picture.

Connect the dots in order.

Spot 4 differences.

How many decorations are left over if each squirrel hangs one on the tree?

Answer: ....

Draw around the toy on each shelf that is different from all the others.

Circle the Christmas card that is not one of a matching pair.

Spot 4 differences.

Find and circle everything on Finty's list.

Finty

Trumpet
Snowglobe
Plane
Boat

Are there more people with teddy bears or dolls?

Answer: ....

Find and circle Millie the fairy.

She has a bow in her hair...

...a wand...

...and she is wearing blue.

Draw a line from each present to the toy that was inside it.

Lead Harley to Conor so they can finish their snowman.

Conor

Harley

Circle the photo that Danny took with his camera.

Danny

A

B

C

Spot 4 differences.

Finish making patterns on these winter clothes for Santa.

Circle the penguin that is not one of a matching pair.

Fill in all the shapes that have purple dots.
What do you see?

48

Find and circle these things in the big picture.

Draw a line along the path
with the fewest snow
monsters.

Draw around these two groups in the picture below.

1.

2.

Lead the Wise Men to the town of Bethlehem.

How many berries are left over
if each bird eats two?

Answer:

....

Connect the two sets of dots in order.

Draw around the Christmas cookie that is not one of a matching pair.

Circle the piece that will finish the picture.

Spot 5 differences.

Find and circle...

...four balls

...three stockings

...two teddy bears

...and seven candy canes.

Find the hidden words. They may be written across or down. One has been found for you.

p (b e l l s) r f h
r j r s n h e m s
e l o d b r i w a
s t o c k i n g c
e t f k q w d z k
n c h i m n e y p
t s a n t a e c a
s l e i g h r x s

bells ✓   Santa   presents
roof   sleigh   reindeer
sack   chimney   stocking

Circle the plug that is connected to the lights on the tree.

A B C

Santa's reindeer have escaped. Can you find and circle all nine?

Lead the train to the station. It can't go past snow on the track.

Find and circle the Hill family's
Christmas lodge.

The Hill family

The lodge has a chimney...

...a decoration on the door...

...and a red roof.

Spot 5 differences.

Find and circle...

...a pair of slippers

... two starfish

...two cupcakes

...a kite

...and three yellow ducks.

Circle the decoration that is not one of a matching pair.

Draw a line from Indy to Violet without touching the holly.

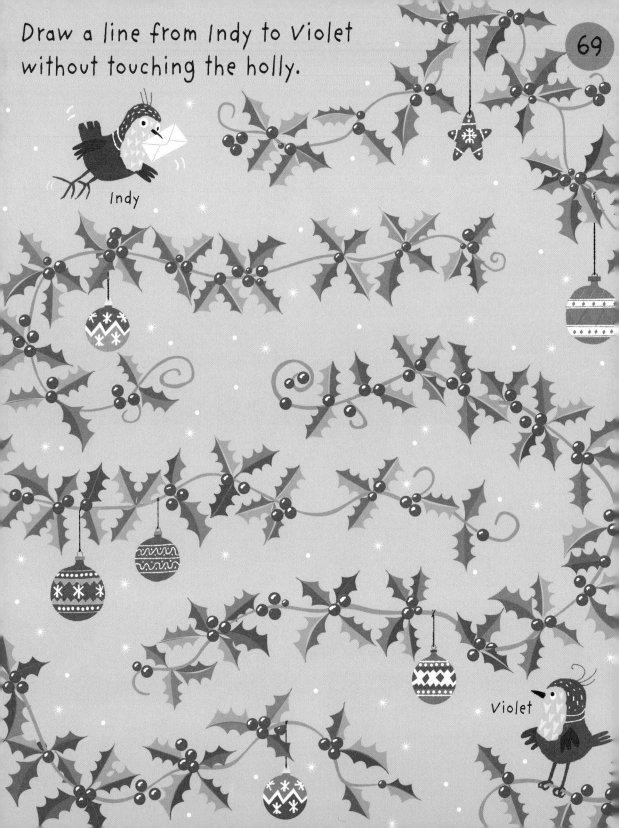

Indy

Violet

Connect the sets of dots in order.

70

Are there enough presents for each mouse to have one?

Answer:

....

Draw around the things you do not need to go skiing.

Are there more cats with
Christmas hats or without?

Answer: ....

Circle the picture that shows the same houses with no snow.

A

B

C

Find and circle three toys that are the same.

Find the hidden words. They may be written across or down. One has been found for you.

```
g  l  z  m  e  c  a  r  d
a  f  r  v  p  a  t  i  z  t
r  m  x  e  l  n  l  c  i  a
l  i  v  p  s  d  i  w  y  r
a  h  o  l  l  y  g  s  j  k
n  f  j  b  n  c  h  e  o  m
d  e  c  o  r  a  t  i  o  n
r  s  t  t  i  n  s  e  l  k
p  v  t  r  e  e  d  a  k  r
```

star ✓   holly   garland
tree   lights   candy cane
cards   tinsel   decoration

Fill in all the shapes that have green dots.
What do you see?

Lead Nick around the park so he passes every star but does not go the same way twice.

Nick

Spot 5 differences.

Circle the Christmas tree that matches the picture on the board.

Draw more presents so that each elf has six.

Find and circle three owls that look the same.

Find and circle...

...six unopened presents

...four marbles

...a robot

...and a gold star.

Lead Santa to the runway. His sleigh must go over arrows in the way they are pointing.

RUNWAY

Find and circle these things in the big picture.

Connect the sets of dots in order.

Circle the piece that will finish the picture.

Each elf must wrap the same number of toys. How many toys is that?

Answer:

....

Find and circle...

...four round windows

...three cats

...a sack of
letters

...five Christmas trees

...and two cars.

90

Spot 5 differences.

Follow the trails to see which fairy will place the star on top of the tree.

Find and circle Mary's snowman.

Mary

It has a carrot for a nose...

...a woolly hat

...and a red scarf.

Draw a line between each pair of matching sweaters.

Draw around these two groups in the picture below.

1.

2.

Answers

1 Answer: B

2

5

9

3 Answer: Elf hats

4

6

10

7

11

8 Answer: Yes

Answers

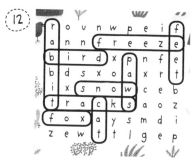

12

r	o	u	n	w	p	e	i	f
a	n	n	f	r	e	e	z	e
b	i	r	d	x	p	n	f	t
b	d	s	x	o	a	f	r	e
i	x	s	n	o	w	r	e	o
t	r	a	c	k	s	e	o	z
f	o	x	a	y	s	m	o	i
z	e	w	t	t	l	g	e	p

13

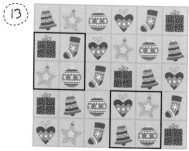

14

15

16

17

18

19

20

21 Answer: Stripes

22

23 Answer: Rabbits

25

Answers

26

27

28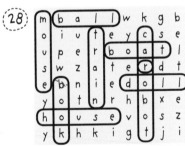

29

30

32

33

34

35 Answer: Two

36

37

38

39

Answers

40 Answer: Dolls

41

44 Answer: C
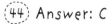
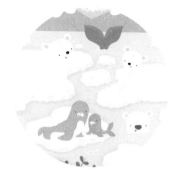

49

42

45

47

43

48

50

51

52

Answers

53 Answer: Three

54

55

56

57

58

59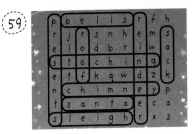

60 Answer: C

61

63

64

65

66

67

Answers

(68)

(74) Answer: B

(75)

(79)

(80)

(70)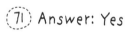

(76)

(81)

(71) Answer: Yes

(72)

(77)

(73) Answer: With hats

(82)

(78)